DISNEP BEDTIME STORIES

Say What?

A __*Bunch*__ of __*Silly*__
   ADJECTIVE   NOUN

Fill-In Stories

Adapted by Avery Scott
Based on the Screenplay by Matt Lopez and Tim Herlihy
And the Story by Matt Lopez
Executive Producers Adam Shankman, Jennifer Gibgot,
Garrett Grant, Ann Marie Sanderlin
Produced by Adam Sandler, Jack Giarraputo,
Andrew Gunn
Directed by Adam Shankman

DISNEP PRESS
New York

Need a refresher course on what to say? Here's a list of what's what in the world of grammar!

An adjective helps describe a person or a thing. Some examples are: **scary**, **hairy**, **squishy**, and **cool**.

To explain how something is done, use an adverb. Just a hint, they usually end in -ly. Some examples are: **wildly**, **quickly**, **loudly**, and **sharply**.

A noun is a person, place, or thing. Pretty simple, huh? Some nouns to keep you on track are: **troll**, **horse**, **rocket**, and **castle**.

If you want to put some action into the stories, you need to use a verb. Some examples are: **run**, **jump**, and **play**. Verbs can also be in the past tense, such as **raced**, **battled**, and **won**. Or they can end in -ing, such as **riding**, **shouting**, and **raining**.

What are you waiting for? Put on your thinking cap, grab a pencil, and let's go!

Say What?

A _Bunch_ of _Silly_
ADJECTIVE   NOUN

Fill-In Stories

First Edition

1 3 5 7 9 10 8 6 4 2

Library of Congress Catalog Card Number 2008933655
ISBN: 978-1-4231-1579-3

For more Disney Press fun, visit www.disneybooks.com
Visit movie Disney.com/BedtimeStories

Before beginning any ___stupid___ story, a good
ADJECTIVE

storyteller must be sure the ___monkeys___
PLURAL NOUN

are prepared. All of the ___elephants___
ANIMAL (PLURAL)

should be ___quickly___ seated and have used
ADVERB

the ___ZOO___. Now if you pay close
PLACE

attention, you'll notice that clouds begin to resemble

___Tatia___ and a(n) _____,
PERSON IN ROOM   NOUN

and you will hear the faint sound of _____
PLURAL NOUN

in the distance. Then, the story begins with the

_____ phrase . . . once upon a _____!
ADJECTIVE   NOUN

5

SUNNY VISTA

Brand New!

_____ visit us at the Sunny Vista Motel.
VERB

All the _____ conveniences, including hot
ADJECTIVE

_____ and _____ television
TYPE OF FOOD   **COLOR**

and _____ conditioning in every _____!
NOUN   **PLACE**

Located on the corner of Sunset and La

_____ Boulevards.
SILLY WORD

Established _____
YEAR

I have put my _____ and soul
PART OF THE BODY

into making the Sunny Vista the very

_____ hotel in _____. I
ADJECTIVE   **PLACE**

believe that making my _____ feel
PLURAL NOUN

_____ is what is most important in a hotel.
ADJECTIVE

Not like some of these new _____ that
PLURAL NOUN

are only concerned with one thing; making a quick

_____. People say my_____ ideas
NOUN   **ADJECTIVE**

about hospitality are great, and they might just be right.

But all my _____ hasn't helped. The Sunny
ADJECTIVE

Vista is on its last _____.
PART OF THE BODY (PLURAL)

Mrs. Dixon's Honeymoon

I can't believe I'm married! I'm staying here at

the _____ Sunny Vista with my new
       ADJECTIVE

husband—it's like a _____ come true. We
           NOUN

_____ up in our _____ with
VERB (PAST TENSE)   **NOUN**

_____ written across the back. Everything
SILLY WORD

looks so _____! Marty, the owner, checked
      ADJECTIVE

my   husband and I in this morning, and we   met

_____ little Skeeter, his son. He was dressed
  ADJECTIVE

in the outfit of a(n) _____! I think our stay
      OCCUPATION

at the Sunny Vista will be just _____.
          ADJECTIVE

My son, Skeeter, is quite the _____ little
                                       ADJECTIVE

_____ that's for sure! He's forever
NOUN

_____ around this motel with _____
VERB ENDING IN "ING"   **ADJECTIVE**

ideas for how to improve it. Just last night he told me

we should put _____ in each room
                ARTICLE OF CLOTHING (PLURAL)

because _____ always forget to bring their
          PLURAL NOUN

own when they _____! I'm sure one day he'll
          VERB

be in charge of this _____ establishment,
                  ADJECTIVE

just like his dear old dad.

My two _____ couldn't be more different
　　　　　PLURAL NOUN

from one another. Little Wendy is quite the book

_____. She's constantly _____
　　NOUN　　　　　　　　　　　VERB ENDING IN "ING"

while her brother makes _____. I find
　　　　　　　　　　　　　PLURAL NOUN

her with books like *Adventures in* _____ and
　　　　　　　　　　　　　　　　　NOUN

Encyclopedia _____. I imagine she'll
　　　　　　　COLOR

grow up to be a(n) _____ or maybe a(n)
　　　　　　　　OCCUPATION

_____. *I* personally think my Wendy would
DIFFERENT OCCUPATION

make a(n) _____ teacher.
　　　　　ADJECTIVE

Wendy's Lament

My baby brother, Skeeter, is such a(n) _____

NOUN

maker! Last week he rode his _____ over

VEHICLE

a(n) _____ and straight into the motel pool!

NOUN

Then, yesterday, Skeeter built a wall made of motel

_____ and _____ through it

PLURAL NOUN   **VERB (PAST TENSE)**

wearing a(n) _____ and carrying

ARTICLE OF CLOTHING

a(n) _____! And just this morning, my father

NOUN

found Skeeter in the motel's _____

NOUN

machine dressed as _____. Being his older

CELEBRITY

sister is so much work!

Skeeter's Favorite Storyteller

My dad is the best storyteller in _____!

PLACE

Every night when he tucks me into _____, he

NOUN

tells me a bedtime story to help me _____ asleep.

VERB

It's almost like he becomes the _____

PLURAL NOUN

in his stories, he tells them so _____.

ADVERB

His stories are about _____ and

ANIMAL (PLURAL)

_____ and even _____ who

PLURAL NOUN   OCCUPATION (PLURAL)

_____! I want to be just like my dad when I grow

VERB

up: the ultimate storyteller and the _____

OCCUPATION

of the Sunny Vista!

Marty's Surrender

Today was a _____ day. I agreed to
               ADJECTIVE

_____ the Sunny Vista Motel to a _____
VERB   **NOUN**

by the name of Barry Nottingham. I know he's right—

the motel is _____ in _____
             VERB ENDING IN "ING"   **COLOR**

ink and there is no way for me to save it. The

_____ news is he promised to let Skeeter be the
ADJECTIVE

_____ of the new motel when he grows up.
OCCUPATION

I guess once the motel is sold, I'll finally have time to

_____, just like I always dreamed!
VERB

NEW AND IMPROVED

Report by _____
NAME OF PERSON IN THE ROOM

The next big _____ has finally been completed
NOUN

and is now taking guests. The Sunny Vista Nottingham,

located in the most _____ and _____
ADJECTIVE **ADJECTIVE**

neighborhood in _____, features exclusive
PLACE

_____ that offer more than just a good night's
PLURAL NOUN

_____. The Sunny Vista Nottingham is owned
VERB

by Barry Nottingham of _____ Industries and
SILLY WORD

was designed by architect _____
CELEBRITY

and interior designer _____. The
PERSON IN ROOM

Sunny Vista Nottingham: It is _____ redefined.
ADJECTIVE

A Thought from Skeeter

In the _____ years since my pop sold
          NUMBER

the Sunny Vista, a whole lot has changed. I still

_____ here, but these days, I do more
   VERB

_____ scraping and _____
TYPE OF FOOD   **NOUN**

changing than _____. My current job
              VERB ENDING IN "ING"

title: _____. Before this, I parked
       OCCUPATION

_____ as a valet and brought
PLURAL NOUN

_____ and the occasional _____
TYPE OF FOOD   **NOUN**

to guests' rooms as a waiter. It's not always a(n)

_____ job, but some _____
  ADJECTIVE   **NOUN**

has got to do it!

★ Mrs. Dixon I.D.s a Thief ★

Skeeter still takes the best care of all the

_____ at the hotel, just like his
    PLURAL NOUN

father taught him. His father filled this motel with

_____, you know. For example,
    PLURAL NOUN

it was not I who stole the juice that belonged to

_____, but rather, the little man with
    CELEBRITY

_____ hair and a(n) _____. He was
   COLOR   **NOUN**

wearing a(n) _____ _____
             COLOR   **ARTICLE OF CLOTHING**

with the hat of a(n) _____ and stood just
            OCCUPATION

_____ inches tall. Skeeter believes me.
  NUMBER

16

Wendy's Wish

Life around here has gotten quite _____
ADJECTIVE

recently. At the moment, there are about _____
NUMBER

_____ in my house, riding
PLURAL NOUN

_____ and throwing _____
ANIMAL (PLURAL)   PLURAL NOUN

for my daughter, Bobbi's, birthday. I wish I could enjoy

it, but I just learned that they are _____
VERB ENDING IN "ING"

down the school where I _____. So now
VERB

I've got to find a new _____ and a new
NOUN

place for me and my kids to _____. I really hope
VERB

_____ is going to help me out!
PERSON IN ROOM (MALE)

17

Bobbi's Birthday

It's my birthday, and my _____ has thrown
FAMILY MEMBER

this _____ party for me, but I don't really
ADJECTIVE

like _____. I'd rather _____ by
PLURAL NOUN   VERB

myself most of the time. Plus, Mom's made her usual

"healthy" _____! There is even a
TYPE OF FOOD (PLURAL)

_____ -free _____ birthday
ANIMAL   SILLY WORD

cake. It's kind of _____ so the other
ADJECTIVE

_____ aren't _____ at all.
PLURAL NOUN   VERB ENDING IN "ING"

Maybe she'll suprise me with _____.
NOUN

Gluten-Free Wheatgrass Cake Recipe*

1 stick softened organic _____
NOUN

½ cup organic evaporated _____
LIQUID

_____ organic eggs
NUMBER

2 teaspoons _____-free vanilla extract
SILLY WORD

1 ¼ cups _____ rice flour
COLOR

1 teaspoon_____ powder
VERB ENDING IN "ING"

½ cup wheatgrass _____
LIQUID

Preheat oven to _____. Mix ingredients
NUMBER

_____ and _____ into
ADVERB   VERB

8-inch pan. _____ for 45 minutes or until
VERB

_____.
COLOR

*These recipes are for fill-in fun only. Do not make them at home.

Suprise for Skeeter?

Wendy asked me to _____ to her house today

VERB

for Bobbi's birthday. I haven't been over there in

_____ years—not since she married that

NUMBER

_____ guy. He and I _____ at

ADJECTIVE   VERB (PAST TENSE)

their _____ party because he was acting

HOLIDAY

like a(n) _____! Anyway, that didn't go

ANIMAL

over _____, so I haven't been invited back.

ADVERB

Until today, that is. I _____ why? Is she ready

VERB

to forgive me?

First Impression

This _____ guy came to my sister Bobbi's
          ADJECTIVE

birthday party today. He asked if we remembered

him and called himself Uncle _____.
                                  SILLY WORD

Then, he tried to _____ Bobbi's birthday
                      VERB

_____ to me, and I had to tell him I was
      NOUN

Patrick, not Bobbi. Real _____. Next, he started
                            ADJECTIVE

_____ about what it's like to have my
VERB ENDING IN "ING"

mom as our _____ at school. He's a little
                OCCUPATION

_____, but I think I could really like him.
      ADJECTIVE

Well, I've done it! I've gone and asked Skeeter to

_____ my kids for me—for _____
VERB   NUMBER

entire days! He's already suggested taking them

_____, but Patrick doesn't
VERB ENDING IN "ING"

_____ well. He offered to teach them to
VERB

play _____—but I would never allow that! I
SILLY WORD

wouldn't normally ask my _____ brother
ADJECTIVE

for help, but I'm _____. And he can't do
ADJECTIVE

too much _____ in such a short time—can he?
NOUN

 22

Jill Meets Wendy's Brother

I can't believe the nerve of some people

_____ up _____ parking
VERB ENDING IN "ING"   NUMBER

spaces. Wendy's _____ parked his beat-up
                    NOUN

_____ truck smack in the middle of
ADJECTIVE

the _____. What was he thinking?! When
       NOUN

I asked him to move it, he mumbled something

about a cushion of _____, and then told me
                       NOUN

I was _____ his! It's going to be a(n)
      VERB ENDING IN "ING"

_____ week if I have to help him with
ADJECTIVE

Bobbi and Patrick.

Skeeter's Cheer for Barry Nottingham

Is this thing on? _____,
VERB ENDING IN "ING"

_____ , one, two, three . . .
VERB ENDING IN "ING"

Okay, when I say Barry, you say _____.
SILLY WORD

Got it? Go!

Barry!

_____!
ANIMAL

Barry!

_____!
PLURAL NOUN

Barry!

_____!
EXCLAMATION

Well, that's not exactly how it goes . . . but

_____ try.
ADJECTIVE

A Germaphobe!

I can no longer _____ with others. It's simply
                    VERB

too _____, what with the _____
      ADJECTIVE   **NUMBER**

germs per square inch on a(n) _____ hand.
                                  ANIMAL

One must respect germs and how _____
                                  ADJECTIVE

they can be when not properly feared. I have taken

to wearing _____ made from
            ARTICLE OF CLOTHING (PLURAL)

_____ and frequently _____ in
  NOUN   **VERB ENDING IN "ING"**

darkened _____ rooms in order to reduce
          ADJECTIVE

their numbers.

The Sunny Vista Nottingham Hotel

Get ready _____.
PLACE

Hotel kingpin Barry Nottingham's latest project will

_____ your _____. Check it out!
VERB — — — — **NOUN**

• The largest _____ on the West _____
NOUN — — — **NOUN**

•1,800 _____
PLURAL NOUN

• _____ restaurants
NUMBER

• 6 _____-style _____
COUNTRY — — — **SILLY WORD**

• 3 _____ areas
VERB ENDING IN "ING"

Doors _____ in late _____
VERB ENDING IN "ING" — — **YEAR**

Do you have your reservation yet?

The old _____ gave me the manager job. I've
NOUN

earned it, that's for sure. For _____ years I've
NUMBER

been _____ around this hotel answering
VERB ENDING IN "ING"

to his every _____ and _____. I
NOUN   NOUN

even started dating his _____ to give myself
NOUN

a(n) _____ up. But, it looks like all of my
NOUN

_____ work has finally paid off. I'll be the
ADJECTIVE

_____ at California's largest hotel. Maybe
OCCUPATION

now I can ditch the _____ that work here,
PLURAL NOUN

except _____, that is.
PERSON IN ROOM

27

Skeeter's Outrage

I can't believe this. That _____ gave Kendall the

NOUN

job as _____—*my* job as _____.

OCCUPATION SAME OCCUPATION

The one I have been waiting _____

NUMBER

years for. In the same breath, I managed to put

my _____ in my mouth by

PART OF THE BODY

calling Nottingham a _____ in

SILLY WORD

front of his daughter, _____. Then, I

TYPE OF FLOWER

called his daughter, _____ and kind

SILLY WORD

of sort of said she spends too much time hanging

out at _____with lots of different

PLACE

_____. Real smooth, Skeeter!

PLURAL NOUN

Scoop of the Day!

Hotel Heiress to _____ at local university!
                        VERB

_____ say that Violet Nottingham,
PLURAL NOUN

daughter of _____ hotel mogul
                     ADJECTIVE

Barry Nottingham, will be _____ at
                              VERB ENDING IN "ING"

_____ this fall. Her intended major?
      PLACE

_____. The university accepted Ms.
VERB ENDING IN "ING"

Nottingham as the first _____ in their brand-
                              NOUN

new acting program. This comes _____
                                    ADVERB

on the _____ of Barry Nottingham's
         PLURAL NOUN

substantial "gift" to the school. Looks like daddy's little

_____ gets everything she wants!
    NOUN

I feel _____ for poor Skeeter. Old
ADVERB

Man Nottingham promised Skeeter's pop that

one _____ Skeeter would be the
NOUN

_____ of this hotel. Now, Kendall's got
OCCUPATION

the job, and it just isn't _____. All because
ADJECTIVE

Kendall is dating Violet. She's so _____ and
ADJECTIVE

_____. Kendall doesn't deserve her. Anyway . . .
ADJECTIVE

wait, was I supposed to be _____ this
VERB ENDING IN "ING"

_____ pizza somewhere?
ADJECTIVE

Chef Albert's French Fried Potatoes*

- 4 medium russet _____
  PLURAL NOUN

- 2 tablespoons _____
  LIQUID

- 1/4 cup chopped fresh _____
  ANIMAL

- _____ garlic cloves, minced
  NUMBER

- _____ salt
  ADJECTIVE

Preheat _____ to 425°F. Cut _____
NOUN   **SAME PLURAL NOUN**

lengthwise into _____-inch-thick slices. Toss
NUMBER

_____ in _____. Bake until deep
ADVERB   **SAME LIQUID**

_____. Transfer to a(n) _____ and
COLOR   **NOUN**

_____ with _____, garlic, and salt.
VERB   **SAME ANIMAL**

*These recipes are for fill-in fun only. Do not make them at home.

Kendall and I have been dating for about _____
NUMBER

months now, and he's _____ and whatnot.
ADJECTIVE

But, he seems to want to change me—to make me

more _____, like him. He insists that
ADJECTIVE

I'll be a "new" Violet _____. He doesn't want
ADVERB

me to _____ or be photographed by the
VERB

_____. So, I've taken to sneaking out to
PLURAL NOUN

_____ like the "old" Violet. Shhh—don't tell him!
VERB

He would _____ out!
VERB

I get asked to babysit for my little _____, just like
PLURAL NOUN

Skeeter does for his sister's kids. It's a _____
ADJECTIVE

time. One of the kids is named _____ and
CELEBRITY

the other is _____. They
NAME OF PERSON IN THE ROOM (FEMALE)

are _____ and _____ years old. They
NUMBER _NUMBER_

enjoy _____ with my _____ the
VERB ENDING IN "ING" _ANIMAL_

most. They style it using _____, _____, and
PLURAL NOUN _LIQUID_

beads. They make me dress up like a(n) _____,
NOUN

too. I _____ around the house chasing them,
VERB

saying _____ and _____! They dig it.
SILLY WORD _EXCLAMATION_

Skeeter's Wheels

My wheels aren't the most _____ or the most
                          ADJECTIVE

_____ for that matter. I drive a huge,
      ADJECTIVE

_____, _____, old _____
    COLOR   **ADJECTIVE**   **NOUN**

that belongs to the hotel. If it gets scratched, my salary

gets _____, so I handle it with care. My
     VERB (PAST TENSE)

wheels make _____ noises when I start it
              ADJECTIVE

up. It sort of sounds like a(n)_____ choking
                                ANIMAL

on a _____ while trapped inside a cardboard
       NOUN

_____. But it gets me from _____
     NOUN   **PLACE**

to _____!
     PLACE

34

Boring Bedtime?

I can't believe how strict my sister is with these

_____ of hers—they aren't _____
PLURAL NOUN   VERB (PAST TENSE)

to watch television! I found out when I went over there

tonight to _____ them. That _____
              VERB   ADJECTIVE

Jill just shrugged it off and suggested that we play a

_____ or do a puzzle. _____! So I
   NOUN   SILLY WORD

_____ called bedtime. What else was I gonna
   ADVERB

do? Then, as Patrick _____ into bed, he
                        VERB (PAST TENSE)

asked me to read him a bedtime story. But all they had

were books like *Rainbow Crocodile Saves the Wetlands*. . . .

35

Rainbow Crocodile
Saves the Wetlands

Deep in the _____ Everglades, there was
                 STATE

a(n) _____ crocodile named _____.
      COLOR   **PERSON IN ROOM (MALE)**

He _____ in harmony with all of the
   VERB (PAST TENSE)

other _____ in the wetlands, like the
      PLURAL NOUN

_____ and _____. But, the
  ANIMAL   **CELEBRITY**

crocodile had one mortal enemy: _____.
                         PLURAL NOUN

The _____ were _____ in
    SAME PLURAL NOUN   **VERB ENDING IN "ING"**

the ecosystem in which the crocodile lived. Something

had to be done. . . .

Patrick's Pet

I love my guinea _____ more than anything
ANIMAL

in the _____. He's small and _____
PLACE   ADJECTIVE

and _____. We call him Bugsy because his
COLOR

_____ are so _____. I
PART OF THE BODY (PLURAL)   ADJECTIVE

found him in the _____ at _____
ROOM   PLACE

one day, and brought him home with me. At night, Bugsy

_____ up onto my _____. And when he
VERB   NOUN

feels _____, he rings a _____! Then
ADJECTIVE   NOUN

he crawls under a(n) _____ to _____ for
NOUN   VERB

the night. He's my best _____!
NOUN

37

Skeeter's Tale of Sir Fixalot

Long ago, in a faraway land, there was a _____
NOUN

named Sir Fixalot. Sir Fixalot performed many a(n)

_____ deed, like goblin removal, unclogging
ADJECTIVE

_____ from drains, and, of course, catching
PLURAL NOUN

_____. The problem was that Sir Fixalot
ANIMAL (PLURAL)

felt _____. No one appreciated all he did
ADJECTIVE

in the land of far, far away. The _____
PLURAL NOUN

apparently did not value _____ work. And
ADJECTIVE

he was so over it!

Sir Buttkiss

Sir Fixalot had a(an) _____. He was the big
                         NOUN

_____ in the faraway land, and his name was
NOUN

Sir Buttkiss. Sir Buttkiss was _____
                                    ADJECTIVE

-looking. So much so that even the _____
                                    ANIMAL (PLURAL)

of the land told him he was _____. Sir
                              ADJECTIVE

Buttkiss also _____ at a top knight college
              VERB (PAST TENSE)

and spent most of his time _____ out with
                            VERB ENDING IN "ING"

the _____ in the land. Needless to say, he
    PLURAL NOUN

made Sir Fixalot feel _____.
                         ADJECTIVE

Kids in the Kingdom

There were two _____ pages that

ADJECTIVE

_____ in the faraway land, and their names

VERB (PAST TENSE)

were _____ and _____!

PERSON IN ROOM   **CELEBRITY**

Their favorite _____ in all the

NOUN

land was, of course, Sir Fixalot because he allowed them

to climb _____, drive his _____ ,

PLURAL NOUN   **NOUN**

and eat plenty of delicious treats, like fried

_____ and _____. But, only

ANIMAL   **TYPE OF FOOD**

when the pages'_____ was not looking!

FAMILY MEMBER

Bobbi's Ending

Tonight, my Uncle Skeeter _____ us a
                              VERB (PAST TENSE)

_____ at bedtime. At the end of
      NOUN

the story, the hero is _____ in a giant
                        VERB ENDING IN "ING"

_____, and develops a(n) _____
ARTICLE OF CLOTHING   **ADJECTIVE**

case of athlete's _____, and then gets eaten by
                    NOUN

_____. So Patrick and I pointed out that it's
   CELEBRITY

_____ for the hero to _____ in the
 SILLY WORD   **VERB**

end. But, Uncle Skeeter told us that in real life, there

are no _____ endings. He said it was a(n)
            ADJECTIVE

_____ we needed to learn. We changed the
  NOUN

ending anyway. . . .

41

★ The Pages Get Their Way ★

This is how the _____ really ends. Forget about
                       NOUN

the man-eating _____. What actually
                   ANIMAL

happened in the faraway land is that Sir Fixalot was

as cool as a(n) _____. He became the
                  TYPE OF FOOD

_____, Friar Fred drop-kicked _____,
   OCCUPATION   **PERSON IN ROOM**

Mermaid Jillian did a funky _____ move,
                                SILLY WORD

the pages performed the fastest _____
                                   KIND OF DANCE

ever seen, and then it began to rain _____.
                                        TYPE OF FOOD

The end.

Bobbi Changes Her Mind

After Uncle Skeeter tucked Patrick and me into our

_____ tonight, I started to _____. Maybe
PLURAL NOUN   VERB

he's not so _____ after all. I mean,
ADJECTIVE

he does let us eat _____ and as much
ANIMAL (PLURAL)

_____ as we like. Plus, his
TYPE OF FOOD

bedtime stories are pretty _____.
ADJECTIVE

I don't know why he didn't come _____ us for
VERB

so many years, but I would feel _____
ADJECTIVE

if he stuck around for a while. I wonder what kind of

_____ we'll hear about in tomorrow
NOUN

night's story. . . .

_____ Report!
ADJECTIVE

Spotted _____ today at the L.A.
VERB ENDING IN "ING"

_____ spot, The _____,
ADJECTIVE   TYPE OF PLANT

was none other than hotel heiress _____
TYPE OF FLOWER

Nottingham. Ms. Nottingham picked at a plate of

_____ and fried _____
TYPE OF FOOD   TYPE OF FOOD

with a side of _____. As the hotel
LIQUID

heiress exited The _____, our
SAME TYPE OF PLANT

_____ caught her and her _____
OCCUPATION   NOUN

ducking into a _____ sports car, before
COLOR

they zipped out of the parking lot.

Breakfast of Champions*

•1 large, ripe _____, sliced
NOUN

•_____ tablespoons wheat germ
NUMBER

•2 rice _____
PLURAL NOUN

•1 tube toothpaste, _____ flavored
TYPE OF HERB

Between the rice _____, place
SAME PLURAL NOUN

_____ slices. _____ cover with
SAME NOUN   **ADVERB**

wheat germ. Top with _____ toothpaste,
SAME HERB

and serve _____. Can be made up to
ADVERB

_____ days ahead of time and kept
NUMBER

_____ in refrigerator.
ADJECTIVE

*These recipes are for fill-in fun only. Do not make them at home.

Aspen the Enforcer

That _____ Bronson continuously asks
     ADJECTIVE

me to call him _____, but I refuse. I find him to
     SILLY WORD

be _____. Just this afternoon, I requested
   ADJECTIVE

that he _____ fix Mr. Nottingham's
    ADVERB

_____, but he muttered something about having
  NOUN

to watch _____ and _____.
    CELEBRITY   PERSON IN ROOM

(He had the nerve to bring those _____
          PLURAL NOUN

here!) And what part of the word _____
        SAME ADVERB

did he not comprehend?

Violet's Night Out

When I _____ into the lobby of the hotel, I
       VERB (PAST TENSE)

was still wearing my _____ from
                      ARTICLE OF CLOTHING

the night before. The _____ were on to
                        PLURAL NOUN

me, too — they _____ with me all the way to
               VERB (PAST TENSE)

the lobby, before hotel security said _____ and
                                        SILLY WORD

they backed down. I hope _____
                          PERSON IN ROOM

doesn't get wind of this! He doesn't care much for my

_____ behavior!
ADJECTIVE

Skeeter on the Job

I think the old _____ is losing it! When I entered
_____NOUN_____

Mr. Nottingham's room to fix his _____
_____ADJECTIVE

television, it was completely _____. He
_____COLOR

said he keeps it that way so that the _____
_____ANIMAL (PLURAL)

don't reproduce so quickly. _____. Anyway,
_____SILLY WORD

in the process of trying to find his busted telly, I managed

to bump into the _____ and then accidentally
_____NOUN

touched the _____ growing on Mr. Nottingham's
_____NOUN

_____. _____!
___NOUN_____EXCLAMATION

48

Barry's Brainstorm

I cannot believe it! I am positively _____
<u>ADJECTIVE</u>

about this! It has been brought to my attention (by none

other than my _____, Skeeter, that the theme for my
<u>OCCUPATION</u>

newest _____ is old _____!
<u>NOUN</u>   <u>ARTICLE OF CLOTHING (PLURAL)</u>

It seems that there is a chain of _____ who
<u>PLURAL NOUN</u>

have already laid claim to the rock and _____
<u>VERB</u>

idea. Looks like it is back to the _____
<u>VERB ENDING IN "ING"</u>

board for Kendall . . . and now, Skeeter, too. He was

the _____ who saw fit to impart this bit
<u>NOUN</u>

of knowledge to me, after all. I might as well give him a

_____ to _____.
<u>NOUN</u>   <u>VERB</u>

49

Violet: Truth or _____, Patrick?
NOUN

Patrick: Truth!

Violet: How old were you the first time you sang

_____?
POPULAR SONG

Patrick: Never. I won't sing that till I'm _____
NUMBER

years old!

Violet: Truth or _____, Bobbi?
NOUN

Bobbi: _____!
SAME NOUN

Violet: Go up to _____ over there and
CELEBRITY

_____ like a(n) _____!
PLURAL NOUN   VERB

50

I almost had a(n) _____

PART OF THE BODY

attack when I walked into the Sunny Vista to pick

up Wendy's _____ today. They were

PLURAL NOUN

_____ out with Violet Nottingham! She

VERB ENDING IN "ING"

told me she really liked my _____ and

ARTICLE OF CLOTHING

asked where I had _____ it. When I told

VERB (PAST TENSE)

her it was from the _____, I expected her to

NOUN

_____, but she said it was a(n) _____ in

VERB   **NOUN**

the rough! I feel oddly _____.

ADJECTIVE

This is it! My shot at being the hero—the new

_____ at the Sunny Vista Mega Nottingham!
OCCUPATION

After Nottingham realized that Kendall had picked

a theme that was so done you couldn't stick a

_____ in it, Nottingham offered me a
NOUN

chance to come up with a(n) _____ theme.
ADJECTIVE

Let the _____ begin! I'm going to come
PLURAL NOUN

up with something so _____, there's no
ADJECTIVE

way Kendall will be able to top it. I hope he doesn't try

anything _____. I mean, all *is* fair in love and
ADJECTIVE

_____.
NOUN

A Gripe from Skeeter

Ya know, some _____ just can't take

PLURAL NOUN

a compliment. I _____ up to this guy in

VERB (PAST TENSE)

a(n) _____ sports car today and asked

ADJECTIVE

him, "_____?" And instead of just saying, "Oh,

SILLY WORD

_____! It was _____ dollars,"

EXCLAMATION   NUMBER

this guy decides it's a good opportunity to say, "If

you _____ for the rest of your life, take

VERB

the _____ and multiply them by

PLURAL NOUN

_____, you might be able to afford a

NUMBER

_____." Rude!

NOUN

53

Raining Gum Balls

I could not believe my _____.
PART OF THE BODY (PLURAL) I was

sitting in my _____ when a gum
NOUN

ball _____ from the sky and hit me right on
VERB (PAST TENSE)

the _____. Before I knew what
PART OF THE BODY

was happening, it was *raining gum balls*! I have heard

of it raining _____ and _____
ANIMAL (PLURAL)   **ANIMAL (PLURAL)**

before, and even raining _____, but gum
NOUN

balls? Now that I _____ about it, it was
VERB

just like in our bedtime story . . . .

I can hardly stomach the fact that my beloved Kendall

is dating that _____ and conceited,
                    ADJECTIVE

_____. I know he loves _____ .
TYPE OF FLOWER   **PERSON IN ROOM**

He's just dating her to get his _____ in
                                 PART OF THE BODY

the _____ at the new _____. I can't help
    NOUN   **NOUN**

but feel _____ about the whole thing. He has
         ADJECTIVE

pet names for me like love _____
                            TYPE OF DESSERT

and _____ face. How can a girl resist
    TYPE OF FOOD

that kind of charm?

Mickey's Rules

These _____ that Skeeter is
        PLURAL NOUN

_____ for the week sure do have a lot of
VERB ENDING IN "ING"

rules they have to follow! I said to them, "Tell Mickey

the truth, you've never played a _____?"
                                    NOUN

And they haven't because their _____ says
                                OCCUPATION

that video games rot your _____. But
                          PART OF THE BODY

I've been playing them for _____ years and
                            NUMBER

look how _____ I turned out! They have
          ADJECTIVE

also never eaten _____ or _____
                  TYPE OF FOOD   **TYPE OF FOOD**

in their lives. So, now we're _____ by
                              VERB ENDING IN "ING"

Skeeter and Mickey's rules—all fun, all the time!

Brainy Bobbi, Part I

Today, I looked in a(n) _____ to learn about the
                          NOUN

guinea _____. Here's what it said:
         ANIMAL

•A species of _____ belonging to the family
                   ANIMAL

_____ and the genus _____.
  SILLY WORD   EXCLAMATION

•Native to _____ and _____
             COUNTRY   ADVERB

related to several _____ that are
                          PLURAL NOUN

commonly found in _____.
                         PLACE

•Also _____ called the *cavy* after its
           ADVERB

_____ name.
  ADJECTIVE

57

I also looked up the term "storyteller." This is its definition:

storyteller

Main _____: **sto•ry•tell•er**
　　　　NOUN

Pronunciation: _____
　　　　　　　　　　SILLY WORD

Function: _____
　　　　VERB ENDING IN "ING"

Definition:　a teller of _____; a(n)
　　　　　　　　　　　PLURAL NOUN

_____; one who _____
OCCUPATION　　　　　　　VERB

58

Another Skeeter Story

Jeremiah Skeets was beginning to feel _____.
ADJECTIVE

He realized that even in the _____ West,
ADJECTIVE

_____ truly mattered. He did not want to
PLURAL NOUN

be thought of as just a(n) _____ any longer.
OCCUPATION

But Jeremiah's shabby _____ and
ARTICLE OF CLOTHING (PLURAL)

his poor, old _____ were preventing him
ANIMAL

from being someone worthy of a(n) _____.
OCCUPATION

He had to _____—quickly!
VERB

Horse Trader

In order to better his chances of being a(an)

_____, Jeremiah Skeets decided
       NOUN

to trade in his ancient _____ for a new one.
                            ANIMAL

The trader was a(n) _____ fellow dressed
                        ADJECTIVE

in a(n) _____, and who spoke
        ARTICLE OF CLOTHING

a lot about things such as _____. But,
                              PLURAL NOUN

Jeremiah simply wanted a new _____. So,
                                 NOUN

the trader gave him a fancy _____
                               SAME ANIMAL

named _____. Best of all, the new
        PERSON IN ROOM

_____ was free!
       SAME ANIMAL

Damsel in Distress

While riding on his new _____, Jeremiah Skeets

                    ANIMAL

came upon an overturned _____ and _____

                       NOUN   **NUMBER**

hooligans who were _____. They had

                  VERB ENDING IN "ING"

surrounded a(n) _____ woman who happened to

              ADJECTIVE

be the daughter of the _____ man in

                 ADJECTIVE ENDING IN "EST"

the West. To fend off the ruthless _____, the

                         PLURAL NOUN

woman was throwing _____ at them, but still

               PLURAL NOUN

they persisted. That is, until Jeremiah _____

                               VERB (PAST TENSE)

up and saved the day!

A Damsel's Thank You

When that _____ man on the _____
                ADJECTIVE   ANIMAL

came and rescued me from an uncertain fate, I knew

I had to find a way to _____ him. He refused
                              VERB

my offer, just as a(n) _____ of honor should. I
                              NOUN

explained that I am a(n) _____ of considerable
                              NOUN

means. So instead of money, I was _____ to
                                    VERB ENDING IN "ING"

give him a kiss when an angry _____ ran up and
                                    NOUN

kicked my savior right in the_____!
                              NOUN

_____ and _____! I can't believe the
　　EXCLAMATION　　　　　SILLY WORD

_____ luck I had tonight! I went to the
　　　ADJECTIVE

sports-car dealership over by _____ expecting
　　　　　　　　　　　　　　　　　PLACE

to have the _____ give me a free
　　　　　　　　　OCCUPATION

_____ , just like in the story I told Patrick and
　　NOUN

Bobbi. But instead, a man stole my _____!
　　　　　　　　　　　　　　　　　　　NOUN

Serves me right for thinking I could _____ these
　　　　　　　　　　　　　　　　　　　VERB

stories to my advantage. And worst of all, he got my last

_____ bucks!
　　NUMBER

Gossip Exclusive!

It was reported that Brit babe Violet Nottingham was

seen looking for her _____ outside of L.A.
NOUN

hot spot _____ last night. After several run-
SILLY WORD

ins with _____ earlier in the evening,
PLURAL NOUN

Ms. Nottingham was _____. When
ADJECTIVE

backed into a _____ by reporters, the young
NOUN

_____ proved that she's no shrinking violet.
OCCUPATION

A mysterious male_____ pulled out what
OCCUPATION

appeared to be a _____ and _____,
NOUN   VERB (PAST TENSE)

sending the paparazzi running for the Hollywood Hills.

Mickey's Problem

So, I have this problem called SPD. Not to be confused

with SBD, which means _____
WORD BEGINNING WITH "S"

but deadly. (Well, okay, I have that problem, too.) But,

SPD stands for _____ Panic
ANOTHER WORD BEGINNING WITH "S"

Disorder. See, sometimes I wake up and _____
VERB

or yell things like _____. Basically, I'm
SILLY WORD

_____ in my sleep. Doesn't bother me, but
VERB ENDING IN "ING"

it sure seems to _____ everyone around me!
VERB

65

From The Manager's Desk

To Whom It May Concern:

It has come to my _____ that the
                          NOUN

following maintenance _____ have
                              PLURAL NOUN

been neglected as of late. Please see to it that

they are completed _____:
                          ADVERB

•Replace _____.
              PLURAL NOUN

•Fix _____ on the freezer in _____
          NOUN   PLACE

•Repair _____ elevator on the south
                ADJECTIVE

side of _____.
              PLACE

Thank you,

Kendall

That Kendall is worse than a(n) _____
ANIMAL

on _____. He had the nerve to give
TYPE OF FOOD

me a(n) _____ time about helping out
ADJECTIVE

_____ the other night when those
TYPE OF FLOWER

_____ photographers were _____
ADJECTIVE   VERB ENDING IN "ING"

around her. He _____ insinuated
ADVERB

that I was trying to be friends with` her to get in

_____ with Old Man Nottingham!
ADJECTIVE

But what really took the _____ is
TYPE OF FOOD

when he _____ my dad. Kendall
VERB (PAST TENSE)

_____ crossed the _____!
ADVERB   NOUN

I realize that I am merely a guinea pig, but most days

I feel like a(n) _____. These humans
ANIMAL

have dubbed me Bugsy, apparently because my eyes

are quite _____. They keep me inside
ADJECTIVE

a _____ in which they have fashioned a(n)
NOUN

_____ sleeping chamber made from chopped
ADJECTIVE

_____. There is also some sort of carousel
PLURAL NOUN

on which they encourage me to _____ endlessly.
VERB

They have also taken to feeding me _____
TYPE OF FOOD

and sweet, caramelized _____. That is not so
LIQUID

bad. They are quite _____!
SILLY WORD

The Care and Feeding of Bugsy

1. Guinea pigs should have _____ quarters
   VERB ENDING IN "ING"

that are at least _____ inches wide and
   NUMBER

twenty-five _____ deep. Use plenty of
   PLURAL NOUN

nesting _____ to line their space.
   PLURAL NOUN

2. Guinea pigs are _____ stressed, so
   ADVERB

they require careful _____. To pick
   VERB ENDING IN "ING"

one up, place a hand under its _____
   PART OF THE BODY

and pull it close to your _____ so it feels
   PART OF THE BODY

_____.
   ADJECTIVE

3. Feed your guinea pig _____ often.
   TYPE OF FOOD

I just heard a piece of _____ that made my day.
PLURAL NOUN

As it turns out, the _____ on which the new
NOUN

_____ Vista Mega Nottingham will be built
ADJECTIVE

just so happens to be the site of _____
CELEBRITY (MALE)

Elementary School. And guess who happens to

_____ at said school? None other than Wendy
VERB

and Jill, Skeeter's _____ sister and friend.
ADJECTIVE

Those two _____ he's been watching
PLURAL NOUN

this week also _____ there. I can use this to my
VERB

advantage — I'm sure of it!

Skeeter's Rooftop Campout

I wanted to _____ it up a bit for the kids, so
　　　　　　　　VERB

I set up a(n) _____ out on the hotel roof
　　　　　　　　　NOUN

last night. I brought them up there and already had

three _____ bags set up for us.
　　　VERB ENDING IN "ING"

I created a makeshift _____ over which we
　　　　　　　　　　　NOUN

made _____. They had never eaten them
　　　TYPE OF FOOD (PLURAL)

before! We all had a(n) _____ time gazing
　　　　　　　　　　　ADJECTIVE

at the stars and _____ the night away.
　　　　　　VERB ENDING IN "ING"

Wendy's kids are really beginning to _____
　　　　　　　　　　　　　　　　　VERB

on me. . . .

Skeeter's S'mores*

4 _____ , broken into halves
    PLURAL NOUN

2 _____ bars, broken into halves
    CANDY

_____ marshmallows
    NUMBER

Place one half of _____ bar on one
    SAME CANDY

_____ half. _____
SAME PLURAL NOUN   ADVERB

toast marshmallow over a(n) _____
    ADJECTIVE

_____ . Top with second _____
NOUN   SAME PLURAL NOUN

half. Gently _____ together. Enjoy!
    VERB

*These recipes are for fill-in fun only. Do not make them at home.

Stargazing
with Uncle Skeeter

Last night, we _____ on the roof
VERB (PAST TENSE)

together—Skeeter, Bobbi, Jill, and me. We laid

back and looked up at the _____ night
ADJECTIVE

sky. The _____ in the sky made
PLURAL NOUN

_____ shapes. I saw a(n) _____
ADJECTIVE   ANIMAL

in the stars, and another group that resembled a

_____! Bobbi saw a(n) _____, and
NOUN   NOUN

Jill spied _____ that looked exactly like
PLURAL NOUN

Bugsy, the _____. It's incredible what your
ANIMAL

_____ can see when you let them!
PART OF THE BODY (PLURAL)

73

For tonight's bedtime story, the kids asked me for a little

_____ and a little romance. So, that's just
NOUN

what I gave them! I told them a story about Skeetacus,

the greatest of all the _____ in ancient
PLURAL NOUN

_____. Skeetacus was a(n) _____,
COUNTRY   **OCCUPATION**

as well as a(n) _____ warrior. He drove a(n)
ADJECTIVE

_____ better than anyone in _____.
NOUN   **SAME COUNTRY**

And, as in all _____ stories, Skeetacus
ADJECTIVE

was trying to win the _____ of
PART OF THE BODY

the fairest _____ in the land. . . .
NOUN

Luck was with Skeetacus. Before he knew what had

_____, he and the fairest _____ in
VERB (PAST TENSE)   NOUN

the land were _____ in a restaurant—
VERB ENDING IN "ING"

together! In the restaurant were all the mean

_____ that gave Skeetacus a(n)
PLURAL NOUN

_____ time when he was _____.
ADJECTIVE   ADJECTIVE

The _____ took one look at
SAME PLURAL NOUN

Skeetacus's date, and felt very, very_____.
ADJECTIVE

So _____ that they all began to
SAME ADJECTIVE

_____ around the restaurant! They looked
VERB

_____. It was the _____ ending!
SILLY WORD   ADJECTIVE

Greetings from Mom!

Dear _____ and Bobbi,
      CELEBRITY

Greetings from the _____ in Arizona!
                        PLACE

It's _____ here so far, and I think you
     ADJECTIVE

will really enjoy _____ in a place like
                 VERB ENDING IN "ING"

this. I hope that Jill and your _____ are
                                 NOUN

taking _____ care of you, and that you
       ADJECTIVE

are eating all your _____! I have to
                      PLURAL NOUN

admit that I ate my first _____ . . . and it
                           NOUN

was _____. I'll make some vegan ones
    ADJECTIVE

for you two when I am back in _____.
                               PLACE

See you in _____ days!
           NUMBER

Love,

Mom

A Letter from Bobbi and Patrick

Dear Mom,

We felt _____ when we got your postcard
          ADJECTIVE

from _____! We miss you _____.
   PLACE   **ADVERB**

But, Jill and Uncle _____ are taking
           SILLY WORD

_____ care of us. Uncle _____
  ADJECTIVE   **SAME SILLY WORD**

has been telling _____ bedtime stories every night.
        ADJECTIVE

He's kind of _____, but we like him.
        ADJECTIVE

Love,

Bobbi and Patrick

P.S. Bugsy says _____!
      EXCLAMATION

I headed to Las Vegas _____, just to
                        ADVERB

spend the day _____. Skeeter called
               VERB ENDING IN "ING"

me during my _____. He beeped in at the
              NOUN

same time that _____ was walking by
                CELEBRITY

with _____. Skeeter asked if I was the
      PLURAL NOUN

most _____ lady in _____.
      ADJECTIVE   **PLACE**

He's one strange _____! Anyway, don't tell
                  SILLY WORD

_____ what I'm up to. He thinks
        PERSON IN ROOM

I'm in _____. After all, what happens in
        PLACE

Vegas, _____ in Vegas. Right?!
        VERB

78

Jill's Rollerblading Run-in

I was just minding my own _____ earlier,
NOUN

taking a long skate around _____,
PLACE

when some _____ steps right in front of
SILLY WORD

me. I _____ but couldn't
VERB (PAST TENSE)

avoid _____ him! We both
VERB ENDING IN "ING"

_____ to the ground, and I smacked
VERB (PAST TENSE)

my _____. I felt _____ . . .
NOUN   **ADJECTIVE**

until I realized it was Skeeter. I asked him if he was

_____. He responded "_____!"
ADJECTIVE   **EXCLAMATION**

Then we headed to _____ to grab a quick
PLACE

bite. I don't know what came over me.

79

Skeeter's Revenge

After Jill _____ into me on her in-line skates, we
　　　　VERB (PAST TENSE)

headed to _____ to grab lunch. But
　　　PERSON IN ROOM (POSSESSIVE)

you'll never believe it! When we arrived, none other than

_____ and her friend _____
CELEBRITY (FEMALE)　　　　　　　　PERSON IN ROOM (FEMALE)

were inside, eating _____ salads.
　　　　　　　　　　　　ANIMAL

Anyway, I felt _____ and asked Jill to pretend
　　　　　　ADJECTIVE

to be my _____. She hesitated, but then I
　　　NOUN

promised to make her some _____, and she
　　　　　　TYPE OF FOOD (PLURAL)

agreed. I really needed to look _____
　　　　　　　　　　　　　ADJECTIVE

in front of those _____ who tortured me in
　　　　　PLURAL NOUN

high school!

Back in the Day

Ah, the good old _____ . Back at High School
                    PLURAL NOUN

_____ , Mary, and I were quite the Queen
TYPE OF FLOWER

_____ .   I   mean,   we   _____
ANIMAL (PLURAL)   **VERB (PAST TENSE)**

around that school as though we were the hottest

_____ since sliced _____ .
    PLURAL NOUN   **TYPE OF FOOD**

Skeeter was kind of a(n) _____ back then,
                              SILLY WORD

and one time we dumped an entire _____
                                            ANIMAL

farm down his _____ . Another time, we read
              ARTICLE OF CLOTHING

his diary to all of the other _____ . And
                                        PLURAL NOUN

then there was that time . . . .

To: jill@yippee.com

Subject: **Wendy Misses Her Kids**

Attach a file

Dear Jill,

I can't wait to get back to _____ tomorrow
                                    COUNTRY

to see my _____. I've never been away
              PLURAL NOUN

from them for so long, and it's been _____.
                                            ADJECTIVE

But the _____ news is that my interviews
              ADJECTIVE

went _____. I think I really wowed them
          ADVERB

with my _____ skills. I should hear from
          VERB ENDING IN "ING"

them by _____, and I'll know
                      DATE

one way or the other if we are leaving _____
                                                PLACE

to head to _____.
                PLACE

Skeeter Messes Up

After Jill and I left the _____, the
PLACE

_____ opened up, and it began to rain
NOUN

_____ and _____. So, we
ANIMAL (PLURAL)   **ANIMAL (PLURAL)**

_____ under the boardwalk to stay
VERB (PAST TENSE)

_____. I got up the _____
ADJECTIVE   **NOUN**

to ask Jill out, and she agreed. I moved in for the

_____, but then I started off, talking
NOUN

about _____ things happening. It was *so*
ADJECTIVE

uncool! Jill called our encounter a _____ and
SILLY WORD

_____ away.
VERB (PAST TENSE)

83

Skeeter is showing those _____

NOUN

some _____ things this week. I

ADJECTIVE

just caught _____ *and* Bobbi in

PERSON IN ROOM

_____ with shaving cream all over their

PLACE

faces. _____ is only _____

SAME PERSON IN ROOM **NUMBER**

years old, so he seems a little _____

ADJECTIVE

to be shaving already. And Bobbi . . . well, Bobbi's a

_____! Skeeter said he didn't want her

NOUN

to feel _____, so he though he should teach

ADJECTIVE

her to shave, too!

I finally get it! The _____ are the
PLURAL NOUN

ones who make the bedtime stories come true! Now

that I know how _____ the bedtime stories
ADJECTIVE

are, I have a plan to seal the deal on my new job:

_____ at the new _____. I'll just get
OCCUPATION   PLACE

the _____ to say I beat Kendall
PLURAL NOUN

in the story I tell them and then it will _____
ADVERB

happen! There is no way that this _____ will
NOUN

fail on me.

Lost in Translation

Skeeto Bronsonian was the _____ space
<small>ADJECTIVE ENDING IS "EST"</small>

_____ in _____! He was destined
<small>OCCUPATION</small> <small>PLACE</small>

to become the _____ of the new planet.
<small>OCCUPATION</small>

There was just one _____ problem. Every
<small>ADJECTIVE</small>

time Skeeto opened his _____ to
<small>PART OF THE BODY</small>

_____ he sounded like _____! Not
<small>VERB</small> <small>PERSON IN ROOM</small>

at all like the _____ space hero he
<small>ADJECTIVE</small>

truly was. He said things like _____
<small>SILLY WORD</small>

and _____. Skeeto had to have his buddy
<small>EXCLAMATION</small>

_____ for him!
<small>VERB</small>

Release the Glopozoid

In order to rule _____, Skeeto first had to
                    PLACE

_____ a man named Kendallo. Unfortunately
VERB

for Skeeto, a Glopozoid was released on him dur-

ing their _____. Glopozoids are
                NOUN

_____ creatures with _____ limbs,
        COLOR   **NUMBER**

crossed _____, a(n) _____,
        PART OF THE BODY (PLURAL)   **ADJECTIVE**

drooling _____, and a(n)
        PART OF THE BODY (PLURAL)

_____-like _____ that allows it
    ANIMAL   **NOUN**

to _____ with ease. They also make
        VERB

_____ noises.
    ADJECTIVE

How to Escape a Glopozoid

There are several methods one might employ in order

to _____ away from a(n)_____
       VERB   **ADJECTIVE**

Glopozoid:

1. Turn off the _____ switch. The creature will
                  NOUN

_____ fall and resemble a squashed _____.
ADVERB   **TYPE OF FOOD**

2. Bite the creature on its _____. Be sure to hit its
                             NOUN

_____ nerve located above the _____.
NOUN   **PART OF THE BODY**

3. _____ like a(n) _____. Contrary to
    VERB   **ANIMAL**

_____ belief, do not run in a zigzag pattern, as
ADJECTIVE

this will only make the creature feel _____.
                                        ADJECTIVE

Oh-no! It looks like my _____ plan has come

ADJECTIVE

back to_____ me! I should have known

VERB

this would happen! Rather than the _____

PLURAL NOUN

having my space story end _____, they had the

ADVERB

hero killed off—death by _____! They

NOUN

claim they want their story to be _____. They

ADJECTIVE

said it was becasue I told them before that there are no

_____ endings in real life. I doubt I'll ever be the

ADJECTIVE

_____ at the _____ now!

OCCUPATION   NOUN

Now that the kids' bedtime story has ensured that I will

be incinerated _____, I figure it's wise to
                      ADVERB

take some precautions. I went over to the _____
                                              NOUN

section at _____ and found a can of
              PLACE

something that said _____-resistant on it. So I
                       NOUN

_____ it all around, covering myself in the
VERB (PAST TENSE)

stuff. I also picked up some _____, a(n)
                                PLURAL NOUN

_____ detector, and a vat of _____. I
   NOUN   **NOUN**

need to play it _____ if I'm going to survive
                   ADJECTIVE

the day!

Mrs. Dixon's Emergency Call

I heard all sorts of _____ coming from
NOUN

Skeeter's room, so I knocked on the _____
NOUN

to see what was going on. I even said I'd call the

_____ . He said he was _____
PLURAL NOUN   **ADJECTIVE**

and that he'd be over soon to _____ my broken
VERB

_____ . _____! I had spoken to the
NOUN   **SILLY WORD**

_____ lady at the front desk. She told me to
ANIMAL

have my leprechaun _____ the shower, but
VERB

he and I aren't on speaking terms right now, so I can't

ask him. Skeeter will just have to take care of it.

I could hardly believe my _____

PART OF THE BODY (PLURAL)

when Kendall from the Sunny Vista Nottingham

came to see me at _____ today. He sat in

PLACE

my _____ and told me that my school—

ROOM

Wendy's _____ and Bobbi and Patrick's

NOUN

_____ is the site of the _____

TYPE OF BUILDING   ADJECTIVE

hotel! Why didn't Skeeter _____ me? He's

VERB

been _____ all over town, saying that he's

VERB ENDING IN "ING"

going to be the new _____ there, and all

OCCUPATION

the while knowingly _____ our lives. . . .

VERB ENDING IN "ING"

A Recipe for
Kona Coffee Ice Cream*

_____ cups _____ cream
    NUMBER   ADJECTIVE

2 cups whole _____
                  ANIMAL

¾ cup granulated _____
                  NOUN

2 tablespoons instant _____
                  TYPE OF FOOD

Pinch of _____
         NOUN

Combine first three _____ in a(n)
                  PLURAL NOUN

_____ saucepan. Bring to a _____.
ADJECTIVE   VERB

Beat in the _____ and the _____.
         SAME TYPE OF FOOD   SECOND NOUN

_____ until the mixture thickens enough
VERB

to coat the back of a(n) _____ and reaches
                  NOUN

_____ degrees. _____ in the _____
NUMBER   VERB   APPLIANCE

for _____ hours and serve _____!
    NUMBER   ADJECTIVE

*These recipes are for fill-in fun only. Do not make them at home.

Sweet Cribs

_____ ! _____ ! This is _____
SILLY WORD   SILLY WORD   NOUN

TV Cribs reporting to you live from Barry Nottingham's

mansion! Looks like this Brit took his invasion

seriously, with _____ rolling acres in the most
NUMBER

sought-after 'hood in the _____. His crib comes
PLACE

complete with a _____ and an Olympic-sized
NOUN

_____ in the backyard. Nottingham's
NOUN

fridge is stocked with all of life's luxuries, like

_____ and _____. Sweet
PLURAL NOUN   TYPE OF FOOD

livin' for the man and his _____ daughter,
ADJECTIVE

hotel hottie _____ Nottingham.
TYPE OF FLOWER

I _____ around so much at Nottingham's
     VERB (PAST TENSE)

party trying to avoid fire (I didn't want the

_____ story to come true!) that I kind of
POSSESSIVE NOUN

took my _____ off the _____.
          PART OF THE BODY   **NOUN**

I reluctantly accepted some kind of _____
                                              ADJECTIVE

ice cream that tasted like _____ when,
                                  LIQUID

wouldn't you know it, a(n) _____ landed
                                ANIMAL

on my cone. I took a lick, and guess what? The

_____ _____ me right on my
SAME ANIMAL   **VERB (PAST TENSE)**

_____!
PART OF THE BODY (PLURAL)

95

Kendall's Vision

I'm _____, if I do say so myself. Check it out.
ADJECTIVE

The MegaNottingham's Broadway theme includes:

•Some _____ Evening Nightclub.
ADJECTIVE

•My Favorite _____ Shopping Concourse.
PLURAL NOUN

•_____ and Jets Swimming Pools.
ANIMAL (PLURAL)

•The _____ Award Terrace.
PERSON IN ROOM

•_____ staff members, all dressed as
NUMBER

_____.
ANIMAL (PLURAL)

Skeeter's Speech

After Kendall's _____ of a hotel theme tanked

NOUN

with Nottingham, I knew winning the job would be a

piece of _____. Except for one minor issue: my

TYPE OF FOOD

swollen _____! I had an allergic reaction

PART OF THE BODY

to the _____ sting! I couldn't say a word without

NOUN

sounding like a mutant _____. So, Mickey had

ANIMAL

to _____ in and translate my presentation. I

VERB

didn't think he could _____ me, but it

VERB

worked. Everyone was moved, including Mickey—I

even saw a tear in his _____.

PART OF THE BODY

97

It was the most priceless of endings to an otherwise

_____ night. That _____
ADJECTIVE   SILLY WORD

Skeeter stole the new job out from under me, but he

managed to undo it all when out of left _____,
                                                    NOUN

he pulled out a fire extinguisher and sprayed

_____ all over Mr. Nottingham's
          PLURAL NOUN

birthday _____ . . . and Mr. Nottingham
            TYPE OF FOOD

himself! I knew it was only a matter of time before that

_____ showed his true _____.
SILLY WORD   PLURAL NOUN

Now, the job is mine . . . all mine!

The Nerve!

_____! I can't believe Skeeter came to see me
SILLY WORD

today at _____ after what he did. I was really
PLACE

beginning to feel _____ toward him. But
ADJECTIVE

now that I know he's just as _____ as all those
ADJECTIVE

_____-hungry hotel _____,
NOUN   **OCCUPATION (PLURAL)**

I can't stand the sight of him. Just goes to show you

that you can't _____ a _____ by its
VERB   **NOUN**

_____. To think, I nearly let him kiss me under
NOUN

the _____. . . .
NOUN

I have to say that my brother has done some

_____ things in his time, but this whole
ADJECTIVE

tearing-down-our-_____-to-build-a-hotel thing
NOUN

takes the _____. But that's not even what
TYPE OF FOOD

bothers me the most. When I left my _____
PLURAL NOUN

with Skeeter, I was _____ hoping that
ADVERB

he'd rub off on them in a _____ way. But all
ADJECTIVE

he seems to have shown them is that there are no happy

_____ and that the bad _____
PLURAL NOUN   PLURAL NOUN

will come out ahead in the end.

Organic Chili Dogs
à la Wendy*

2 pounds organic ground _____
PLURAL NOUN

1 cup _____
LIQUID

1 large minced organic _____
NOUN

5 ounces _____ sauce
LIQUID

2 tablespoons _____ powder
TYPE OF FOOD

5 tablespoons organic _____ sauce
ANIMAL

1–2 tablespoons ketchup

Simmer ground _____ and _____ for 15
PLURAL NOUN   FIRST LIQUID

minutes. Add remaining ingredients and _____
VERB

for _____ hours. If sauce is not
NUMBER

_____, stir in beaten _____.
ADJECTIVE   NOUN

_____ over organic hot _____.
VERB   ANIMAL

*These recipes are for fill-in fun only. Do not make them at home.

Donna Saves the Day

After running into Skeeter Bronson and his girlfriend

the other day, I got to _____ that
VERB ENDING IN "ING"

sometimes you can do the _____ thing in
ADJECTIVE

life. That's why when he came to see me about blocking

the _____ for this new megahotel, I
NOUN

was happy to _____. As commissioner of
VERB

_____ in this town, I had the power to
VERB ENDING IN "ING"

_____ the _____. So there
VERB   PLURAL NOUN

you have it! Application denied!

Call Cannot Be Completed as Dialed

Well, Skeeter Bronson turned out to be

_____ than I gave him
ADJECTIVE ENDING IN "ER"

_____ for. He set me up with a great new
NOUN

_____ for my hotel. I wanted to halt the
NOUN

demolition of _____ Elementary School.
CELEBRITY

So I immediately dialed Kendall on my _____
NOUN

to tell him the _____. But the call could not be
PLURAL NOUN

completed! Kendall was about to _____ that
VERB

school building to _____! Skeeter ran
SILLY WORD

out of here faster than a _____ being chased by
NOUN

a _____. Hope he gets there in time . . .
ANIMAL

103

Save the Day?

Patrick and I have a(n) _____ plan to
ADJECTIVE

stop the _____ from tearing down our
OCCUPATION (PLURAL)

_____! We are _____
PLACE   VERB ENDING IN "ING"

into the building while none of the _____
PLURAL NOUN

are _____ and we'll hang a huge
VERB ENDING IN "ING"

_____ in the window. We know it will make
NOUN

those hotel people change their _____.
PLURAL NOUN

We just wish Uncle Skeeter were here to

_____ it!
VERB

SAVE OUR SCHOOL!

OUR SKOOL _____.
VERB ENDING IN "S"

SAVE OUR _____!
NOUN

STOP THE _____!
VERB ENDING IN "ING"

EDUCATION OVER

_____!
PLURAL NOUN

KIDS _____, AND
VERB

SO DOES_____!
PLACE

Puppy Love

Patrick and Tricia sitting in a _____.
NOUN

First comes _____,
NOUN

Then come _____,
NOUN

Then comes _____ with a _____
CELEBRITY   ANIMAL

carriage!

106

Jill's Wild Ride

Skeeter and I had to _____ Kendall! But how?
VERB

Then we saw a bunch of bikers at the _____
TYPE OF FOOD

stand, and we had a _____. We jumped on one
NOUN

of the _____, and Skeeter drove like a(n)
NOUN

_____ while I hung on for dear life.
ANIMAL

We drove the _____ way down a(n)
ADJECTIVE

_____-way street. Then, we passed through
NUMBER

a _____ range, and I was nearly hit by
VERB ENDING IN "ING"

golfers. But, luckily, we got to the school in the nick of

_____!
NOUN

21 Marty's Motor Inn

Come on home to Marty's _____ Inn.
NOUN

Take a step back in _____ but with all the
NOUN

conveniences of the _____ life.
ADJECTIVE

Marty's _____ Inn — where the _____ is
SAME NOUN   NOUN

always our top _____.
NOUN

Can't wait to _____ you soon!
VERB

Sometimes life does turn out to have _____
                              ADJECTIVE

endings. And sometimes it doesn't. A cruel twist

of _____ left me in the position of
        NOUN

_____ and Kendall in the position
        OCCUPATION

of _____ . . . at Marty's
              OCCUPATION

Motor _____. Can you believe it!
              NOUN

_____! I muck about doing nothing but
        SILLY WORD

cleaning _____ and picking up after
            PLURAL NOUN

the _____ that stay here. It's positively
        ANIMAL (PLURAL)

_____—even the little guinea _____
    ADJECTIVE   **ANIMAL**

is my superior now.

109

I do declare that my new living arrangements are quite

_____. My captors have me situated in quaint
ADJECTIVE

quarters in a retro _____ inn. I now dine on these
NOUN

marshmallow-and-_____ concoctions—they
NOUN

taste divine. I love to lick the remaining _____
NOUN

from my paws. And I now have my own servant—that

inferior _____, Kendall, who I met not that
ANIMAL

long ago. Sometimes I _____ just to make
VERB

him run in and clean up after me. It's _____!
ADJECTIVE

Write your own
bedtime story!

Use all the nouns, verbs, and adjectives you want to create a unique bedtime story, just like the ones Skeeter, Bobbi, and Patrick tell!

(The story doesn't have to end here!)